Tundra Mouse

A Storyknife Tale

by **MEGAN McDONALD**

illustrated by **S. D. SCHINDLER**

ORCHARD BOOKS

NEW YORK

Yup'ik girls in southwestern Alaska still practice the art of storyknifing, a unique tradition of drawing pictures with the tip of a knife in mud or snow while telling a story. The pictures depict settings and events recounted in the tale. While storyknives of old were made of carved wood, bone, or ivory, ordinary metal table knives are used today, as are sticks, nails, and other pointed objects. The storyknifing symbols that appear in this book are based on figures drawn for us by Elena Charles, a Yup'ik elder who lives in Bethel, Alaska, and to her we are grateful. The author also wishes to thank James Culp of The Film History Foundation in San Francisco and the Kuskokwim Consortium Library in Bethel, Alaska.

—M.M. & S.D.S.

Orchard Books, 95 Madison Avenue, New York, NY 10016

Manufactured in the United States of America
Printed by Barton Press, Inc.   Bound by Horowitz/Rae
Book design by Jennifer Browne

10 9 8 7 6 5 4 3 2 1

The text of this book is set in 16 point Cheltenham.
The illustrations are colored pencil on pastel paper.

Library of Congress Cataloging-in-Publication Data
McDonald, Megan.
Tundra mouse : a storyknife tale / by Megan McDonald ; illustrated by S. D. Schindler.
p.   cm.
"A Richard Jackson book."
Summary: Using a traditional technique called storyknifing,
two Yup'ik Eskimo sisters share a story about the mice that made
a nest out of tinsel from the Christmas tree.
ISBN 0-531-30047-1. — ISBN 0-531-33047-8 (lib. bdg.)
1. Yup'ik Eskimos—Juvenile fiction.   [1. Yup'ik Eskimos—Fiction.
2. Eskimos—Fiction.   3. Mice—Fiction.   4. Storytelling—Fiction.]
I. Schindler, S. D., ill.   II. Title.
PZ7.M478419Tu   1997   [E]—dc21   96-53221

For John Active and Elena Charles of Bethel, Alaska
—M.M.

To Spooky Mousedred for procuring a mouse model
—S.D.S.

One berry ripe
Two berries ripe
Three berries ripe . . .
  "Watch out for mouseholes," Elena
told her younger sister. "You know
what happened last Christmas!"
  "Tell me," Lissie said.
  Elena dug the storyknife from her
inside pocket. The two girls bent
over the muddy banks of the river,
scratching lines in the soft brown
earth. First a mouse, then a mukluk . . .

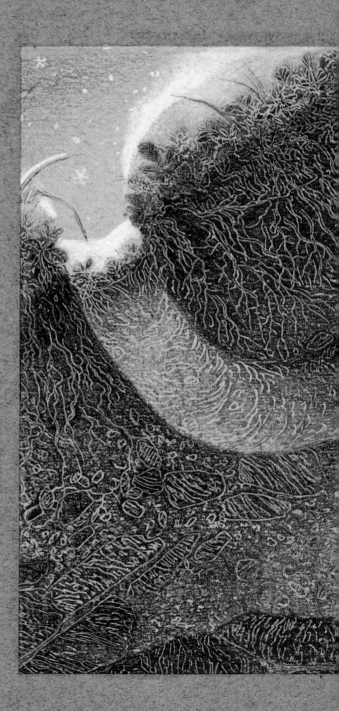

Far, far north, in the land beyond trees, lived Tundra Mouse. Down a long tunnel beneath the snow, deep inside a feather-lined nest, Tundra Mouse spent the winter eating the cotton-grass roots she had stored in nice neat rows.

Po! One day the ground shook and the ceiling caved in. A big furry boot came crashing through, and Tundra Mouse raced out of her mousehole. She scurried for cover to a hiding place dark and safe. Grandmother's gunnysack! It was filled with *unschrut*, the cotton-grass roots Grandmother had been collecting all morning. *Sik sik.* Tundra Mouse nibbled the roots. *Sik sik sik. Zip!* Quick as a shooting star, Tundra Mouse felt the new nest moving.

ZZZZZrrrrrrr! A loud roar. Tundra Mouse peered out a tiny peephole. The Arctic prairie rushed past in a blur. Tundra Mouse was flying!

"But mice can't fly," Lissie said.
"She was riding on the back of
Grandmother's snow-go."

The high-pitched whine stopped. *THUNK!* Tundra Mouse
landed with a crash on Grandmother's kitchen table.

Whisk! Out came the ice-cream-making bowl. *Wak wak
wak wak wak.* Grandmother began chopping the roots
for her Christmas *akuduk.* *Whirr!* She stirred shortening
and sugar with three kinds of berries. *One berry ripe, two
berries ripe, three berries ripe . . .*

Tundra Mouse pawed at the sack's small hole, squeezing herself out. *Mww, mww, mww.* She squeaked with tiny kissing sounds, eating bits of sugar, rolling in flour, and licking the ice cream all around the rim.

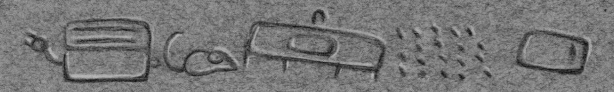

Tundra Mouse leaped to the countertop, skidding on the slick surface. A shiny creature glared at her without blinking. *Sniff, sniff, sniff.* Tundra Mouse scurried up the side. *Aiieee!* Not one mouth, but two! She knew the teeth of a wolverine, but she had never seen the jaws of a toaster. *Eek!* Tundra Mouse raced back down, sliding into a slippery-smooth pit, walls all around her. Rain pelted her head with big drops. She gnawed on a hard white cake in the sink.

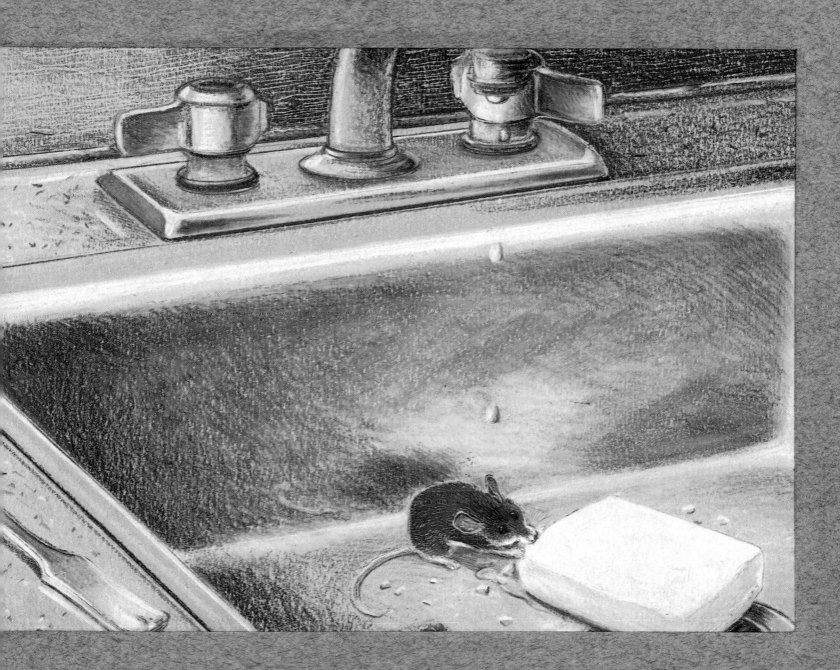

"What was cake doing in the sink?"
"Not cake, silly. Soap!"

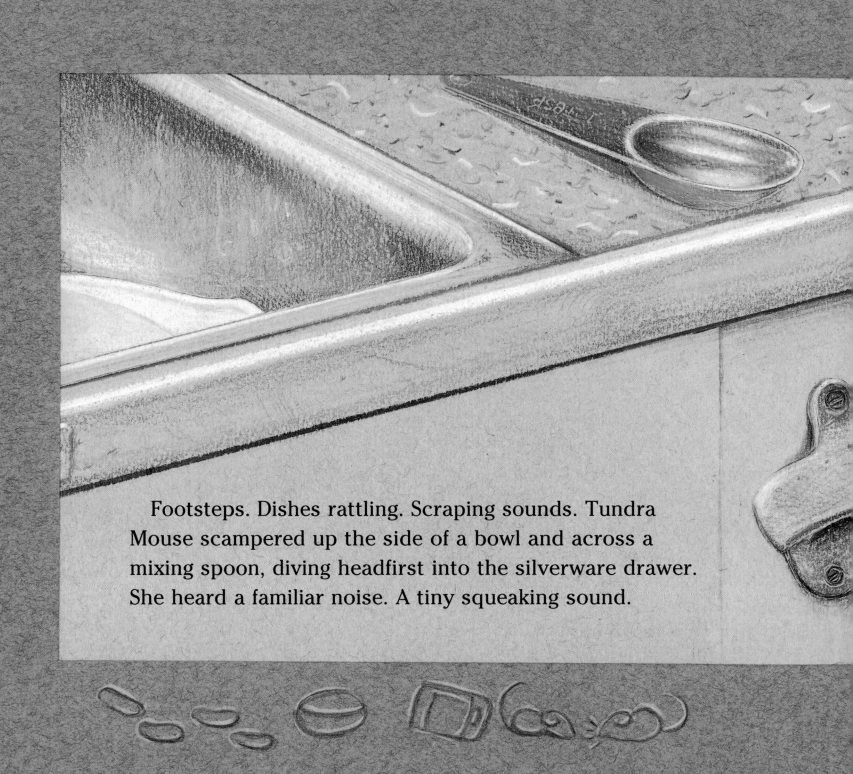

Footsteps. Dishes rattling. Scraping sounds. Tundra Mouse scampered up the side of a bowl and across a mixing spoon, diving headfirst into the silverware drawer. She heard a familiar noise. A tiny squeaking sound.

"Was it another mouse?"
"Yes. We will call him House Mouse."

Mww, mww, mww! The two mice squeaked with high-pitched kissing sounds, sniffing and rubbing noses, twitching whiskers. Just then, a giant hand reached into the drawer. House Mouse squeezed through a small hole, Tundra Mouse at his heels. They raced along dusty pipes and wires to . . . a mouse house inside the wall!

Tundra Mouse stared in wonder at the mess of a nest!
No cushiony carpet of grass. No walls lined with feathers
and musk-ox fur. No nice neat cache of cotton-grass tubers.
Just a terrible tangle of things Tundra Mouse had never
seen before. Bubble gum wrappers, postage stamps, and
half a coffee cup for a bed! Raisins and peanut shells
piled topsy-turvy with pop tops, paper clips, and an old
toothbrush. Even a horn button and three red checkers!

"Those were my checkers that I lost, weren't they? And Grandmother's button. Hurry and tell the rest, Lena. Do you think House Mouse took my jacks too?"

Elena curled her tongue against her front teeth and drew in her breath.

That night, Grandmother dozed in her chair while House Mouse led Tundra Mouse along a secret passageway into the living room. Tundra Mouse recognized a tall spruce, but it was covered with hundreds of blinking eyes. Had the tundra stars fallen to earth? House Mouse scampered in and among the stars, filling his cheeks. The two mice worked all night, spiriting away strands of shiny silver straw.

"I know. I remember! Let me tell!" Lissie picked up a stick and drew a tree in the mud. "Each night, something else disappeared from the Christmas tree."

Christmas morning, we woke up and ran to open our presents. The tree was bare. Not one cookie left, not a single candy cane. Even the bows on our presents were gone! Grandmother told us it was the *cingssiiks*. Tiny magical people who sneak in at night and steal things, she said. We told her we heard scratching sounds in the walls. She said that was the little people. She said if we wished hard enough, the *cingssiiks* would bring everything back. I wished so hard my eyes hurt. And remember? When we came home from the star procession, the tree was like new.

Lissie put her stick down.
"Lena, tell about how it was so
cold our eyelashes froze and we
wore mukluks in the house! Then
the pipes burst!"

Tundra Mouse and House Mouse ate popcorn and rolled
in ribbons and stuffed candy wrappers and cookie crumbs
in the cracks. They were fixing a soft bed for Tundra
Mouse when . . . *Bam! Bam! Bam!* Thunder shook the
walls. *Shhhh!* Rain drenched the mice. *ZZZZZ! ZZZZZ!*
Something with sharp teeth was after them, eating right
through the wall!

Mww, mww, mww! House Mouse let out a high-pitched warning and the two mice ran for their lives—along the pipes and away from the house and across the snow and into the dark, cheeks bulging, feet flying. Tundra Mouse and House Mouse jumped and leaped and chased each other all day, following flocks of snow geese. They ran through the night, under the northern lights, heading straight toward the rising sun, to The Land of Sky. The tundra. Home.

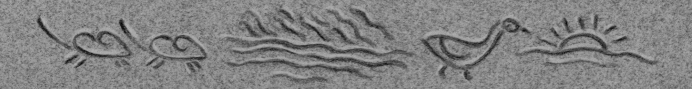

Elena stopped.

"Don't let it be over yet," Lissie said. "Tell the best part. You know. What we found out on the tundra. And don't forget to say 'Wani-watung' like Grandmother. Please, Lena?"

Weeks later, we zoomed out to the tundra on Grandmother's snow-go. She showed us just how to move in circles on our heels, pressing lightly, looking for mouseholes. And to shout, *"Wani-watung! Look, here it is!"* when we found one. I pulled out handfuls of cotton-grass roots and put them in the sack. You stayed behind, leaving cranberries for the mice. *One berry ripe, two berries ripe, three berries ripe . . .*

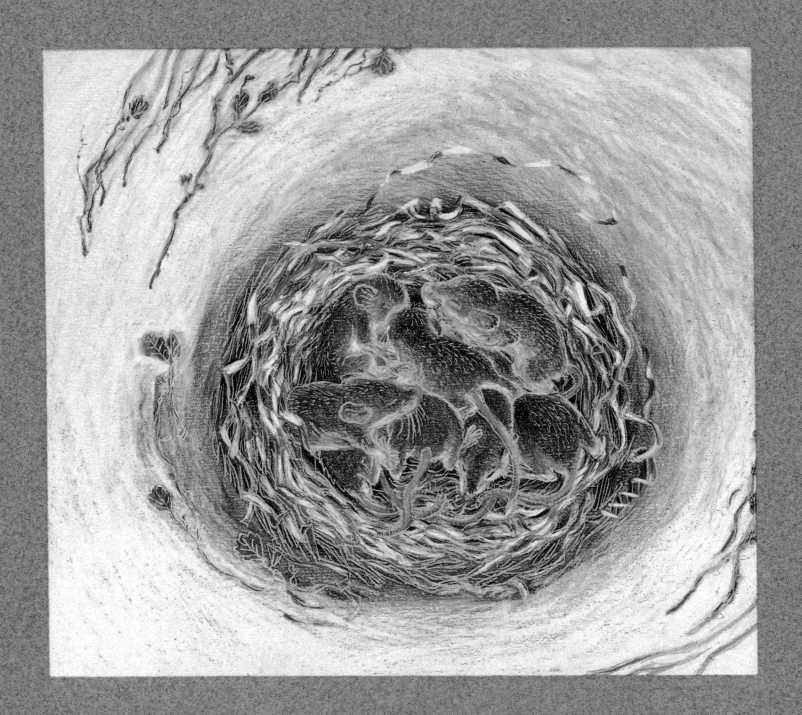

"Wani-watung!" I fell backward, right into a mousehole. Grandmother came running. Inside, we saw a wriggling, squirming, squeaking heap of baby mice making tiny kissing sounds, all snug in a mouse bed soft and round! But their nest was not made of cotton grass. This nest was woven of bright strands of shiny silver straw. Christmas tree tinsel.

"Now can it be the end?" Elena asked.

"Mmmm-hmmm. That story makes me hungry for Grandmother's akuduk. Lena? May I hold your storyknife?"

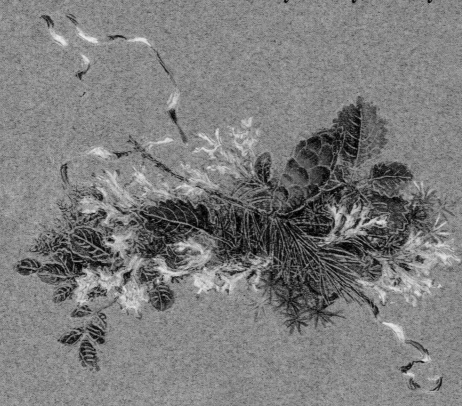

Lissie smoothed the mud until no lines were scratched there. With the tip of the storyknife, she carved a setting sun.

"Just a few more berries," said Elena. "Then it's time to go."

"One more story? Please?"

"It's getting dark. If we don't hurry, Angaayuk will get us. I could tell you that story."

"Never mind. Let's run."